Love Monster
& the Scary Something

Rachel Bright

HarperCollins *Children's Books*

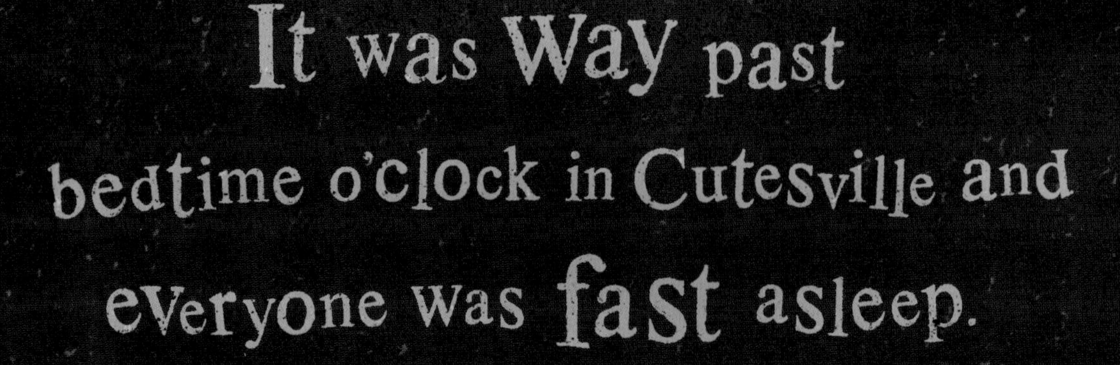

It was way past bedtime o'clock in Cutesville and everyone was fast asleep.

Everyone, that is,
except one particular monster.

(Hello, Love Monster.)

You see, just like every night, he'd made a cup of hot milk with chocolate sprinkles...

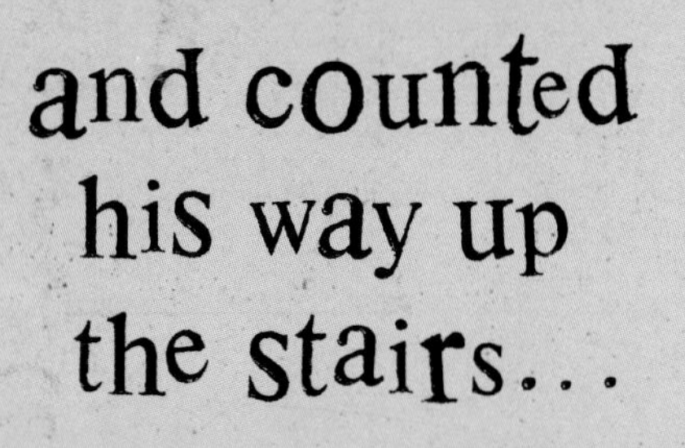

and counted his way up the stairs...

one

two

three

four.

LM

As usual,
he'd read
FIFTEEN AND
A HALF bedtime
stories...

closed his eyes
and snuggled in
tight with teddy.
But that night...

. . .the harder
he tried to nod off,
the awaker he was.

And the later
and darker . . .

and SpoOOokier it got.

So Love Monster lay and listened to
the sounds of the shadowy night.

TICK TOCK TICK TOCK TICK TOCK TICK

That was the clock.

SSSSSSSshhhhhSSSSSSh

That was the song of the wind in the leaves.

Hoo hoooooOOOO hoo

That was the Cutesville Owls.

Rustle-Rustle

That was the...

tOck
hhhhhhh
Hold on!
WHAT...
was THAT???

It sounded like
SOMETHING
in the garden.

NOW it sounded like
SOMETHING downstairs!

BA

"Aaaaaarrg

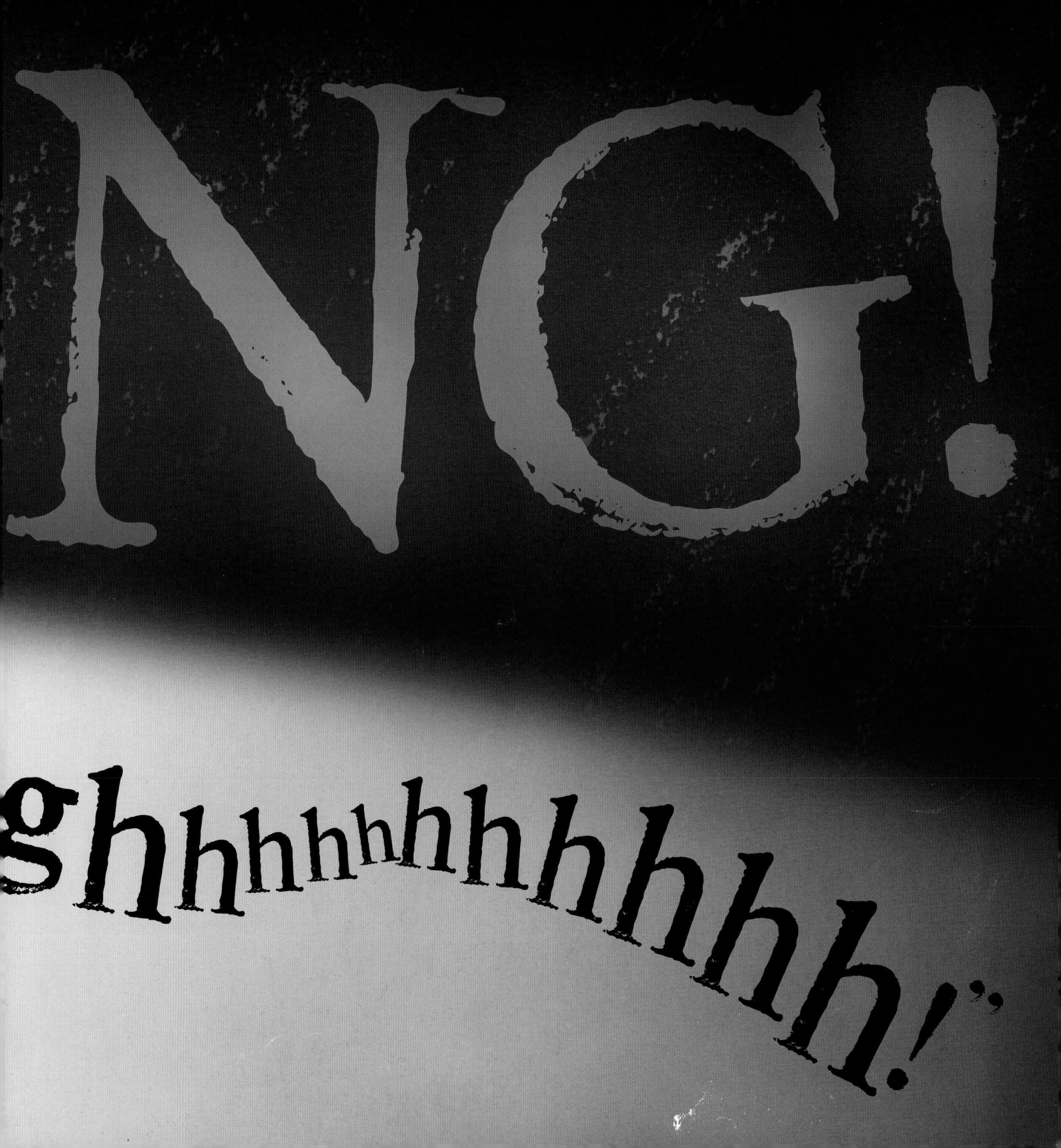
NG!
ghhhhhhhhhhh!"

He dived under the duvet,
his heart beating loud and fast.

There was definitely
SOMETHING
out there!

And that
SOMETHING...

had definitely GOT IN!

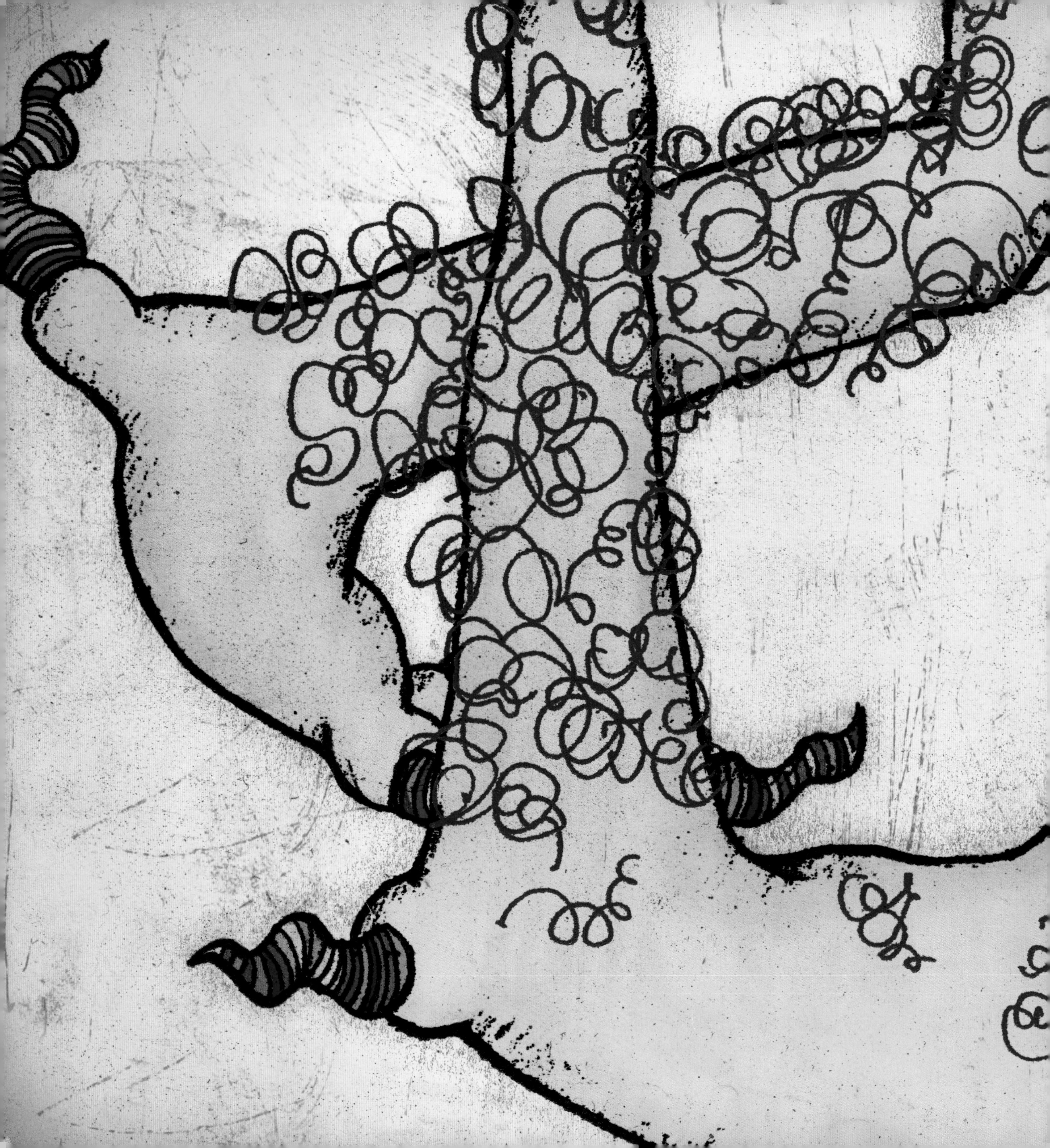

Pittery-pat... Pittery-pat...
Pittery-pat...
oooOOOOoooooh!
It sounded like
THE SOMETHING
had
terrible
twisterly
toenails!

Bump...
Bumpety...
Scuffle-shuffle
BUMP.

Oh NooOOooo!

It sounded like

THE SOMETHING

with terrible twisterly toenails

was coming…

UP…

THE

STAIRS!

Crunch-crunch-crunchety-crunch.

EEEeeeeeK!

It sounded like

THE SOMETHING

with terrible twisterly toenails had

GREAT BIG TEETH.

And it sounded

HUNGRY!

Suddenly Love Monster could bear it no longer. Somehow, hiding from THE SOMETHING outside... got harder than finding something brave *INSIDE*. So he flung back the covers...

flicked on the torch and…

"FffffffneeeeeeEE

EEEEEeeep!"

went THE SOMETHING.

As it turns out, Love Monster.......hadn't been the only one.....

And he wasn't.................the only one........

. . . . . . who couldn't sleep . . . . that night.

. . . . Who didn't want . . . . to be alone.

And as the tiniest, fluffiest bunny in Cutesville explained to his I-suppose-a-bit-googly-eyed friend... they both **laughed** and **laughed** until their tummies ached.

And you know what?

The dark just didn't seem
that spooky any more.

You see, sometimes, it's only when you're brave enough to face what you're afraid of...

that you find out there was
nothing to be scared of, after all.

For my mini-monster-to-be...
May you always find your brave-inside X

First published in paperback in Great Britain by
HarperCollins Children's Books in 2015

1 3 5 7 9 10 8 6 4 2

ISBN: 978-0-00-754032-7

HarperCollins Children's Books is a division of HarperCollins Publishers Ltd.

A CIP catalogue record for this title is available from the British Library.

Visit our website at: www.harpercollins.co.uk

Printed and bound in China